GREAT TALES FROM LONG AGO

RIP VAN WINKLE

Retold by Catherine Storr
Illustrated by Peter Wingham

Methuen Children's Books
in association with Belitha Press Ltd.

Copyright © in this format Belitha Press Ltd., 1984
Illustrations copyright © Peter Wingham 1984
Art Director: Treld Bicknell
First published in Great Britain 1984
by Methuen Children's Books Ltd.,
11 New Fetter Lane, London EC4P 4EE
Conceived, designed and produced by Belitha Press Ltd.,
2 Beresford Terrace, London N5 2DH
ISBN 0 416 49540 0 [hardback]
ISBN 0 416 49110 3 [paperback]
Printed in Great Britain

Note: The story is based on the original
by Washington Irving in *A Writer's
Sketch-book*. It takes place in the American
Colonies in the years 1770–1790. When
Rip wakes up from his long sleep the War
of Independence (1776) is over and a
new nation has been born.

CS

IN AMERICA, MORE THAN TWO HUNDRED YEARS AGO,
there was a man called Rip van Winkle.
He and his family lived in a village
near the great Hudson river and the Catskill mountains.

Rip was a kind man.
He liked talking to his friends in the village inn,
and he liked playing with the children in the village.

HE DID NOT LIKE WORK.
He was not a good farmer.
He did not look after his cows properly,
so they were always lean and dirty.
He did not sow his crops at the right time,
or weed the fields, so he never had good harvests.
Worst of all,
his wife scolded him, night and day for his laziness.
So he spent most of his time with his friends
in the village inn.

ONE DAY, HE COULD NOT BEAR
his wife's nagging tongue any longer.
He took his gun, and Wolf, his dog,
and he went off towards the mountains.
After some time, he stopped on a grassy hill
to enjoy the lovely autumn day,
and to feel how wonderful it was
to be out of reach of his wife's scolding.
Although the sun was shining,
he heard a curious rumbling sound,
which echoed round the hills, like thunder.
Whenever this happened, his dog growled and bristled
as if he smelled danger.

THE SUN SANK LOWER IN THE SKY, AND RIP THOUGHT
that he ought to turn his steps towards his home.
But just then, he heard a voice calling him:
"Rip van Winkle! Rip van Winkle!"
At first he could not see anyone about,
but as the sound became louder,
he saw a strange figure coming towards him.
It was an old man, dressed in old-fashioned clothes
and carrying a barrel on his shoulder.
As he came near, the old man made signs
that he wanted Rip to help him.
So, taking turns at carrying the barrel,
Rip and the stranger climbed up a steep path,
leading to an opening in the rocks above.

When they reached the opening,
Rip saw in front of him an open grassy meadow.
Here several old men were playing at ninepins.
They did not speak, and their faces were very serious.
Now Rip saw that what he had thought was thunder,
was the rumbling sound made by the huge balls
as they rolled over the ground.

As RIP AND HIS COMPANION APPROACHED,
the old men stopped their game,
and turned to stare at Rip.
His companion now signed to him
to help pour wine from the barrel he had carried,
into jugs and mugs, and to pass these
around amongst the players.
Presently, when they had drunk as much as they wanted,
they went back to their game.
Rip saw his chance to taste the wine
he had been serving to the others.
He found it very good.
He drank, and then drank more.
At last his head felt heavy,
and he lay down on the ground to sleep.

WHEN HE WOKE, HE WAS SURPRISED TO FIND
that he had slept for the whole night through.
He was even more surprised to see
that he had been carried back to the grassy hill
where he had been the day before
when he had first met the old man with the barrel.
He feared that his wife would scold him
for staying out all night.
He whistled for his dog to go home with him,
but Wolf did not appear.
He found too, that someone had stolen his gun
and left a rusty, useless weapon in its place.

HE STARTED ON HIS JOURNEY BACK.
But he felt strangely tired and stiff.
It was difficult to find his way,
for there seemed to be trees and streams
where he had not noticed them before.
He was very hungry, so he walked as fast as he could,
but even so it was a long time
before he was within sight of the village.

As he walked along the road,
he met several people he did not recognise.
This surprised him.
He thought he knew everyone living near-by.
He noticed, also, that as the people passed him,
they stared at him, and many of them
put their hands up to their chins.
Rip put his hand up to his own chin,
and found that his beard had grown
down almost to his waist.

AT LAST, HE REACHED HIS OWN VILLAGE STREET.
But there were houses there which he had never seen before.
And here, too, all the people were strangers.
He began to think that he must have lost his way
and come to a village which was not his own.
When he came to his house,
he saw that it was deserted.
The front door stood open. He looked inside,
and saw nothing but empty rooms,
dirt, dust and cobwebs everywhere.

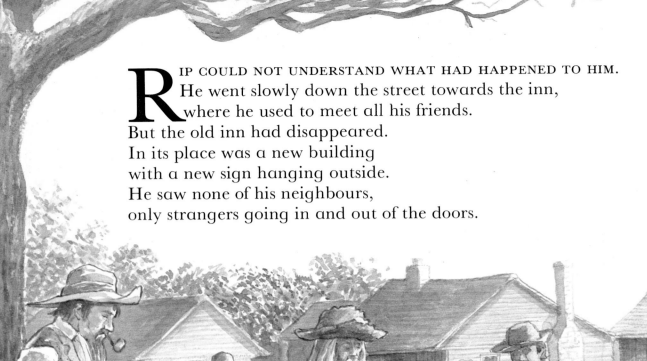

R IP COULD NOT UNDERSTAND WHAT HAD HAPPENED TO HIM.
He went slowly down the street towards the inn,
where he used to meet all his friends.
But the old inn had disappeared.
In its place was a new building
with a new sign hanging outside.
He saw none of his neighbours,
only strangers going in and out of the doors.

By this time, a crowd of men, women and children
had gathered round Rip, and were staring
at his long beard and his curious clothes in surprise.
Rip asked them, "Where are my friends?
Where is Nicholas Vedder, the landlord of this inn?"
"Nicholas Vedder? He died a long time ago.
Who are you?" said an old man in the crowd.

"I'm Rip van Winkle. Don't you know me?"
"You aren't Rip van Winkle.
That's Rip van Winkle over there," the old man said,
and he pointed to a young man on the edge of the crowd.
"But if that is Rip van Winkle, who am I?
Doesn't anyone here remember me?"
Rip asked, in despair.

A young woman with a baby in her arms, said,
"Rip van Winkle was my father.
That young man over there, is my brother.
My father walked out of our house one day,
with his dog and his gun,
and no one saw him again.
But that was twenty years ago, when I was a little girl."
She came up to Rip and looked carefully at him.
"Yes. This is my father," she said.
Rip trembled. "Your mother? Where is she?" he asked.
"Dead. She got furious with a pedlar
and died in a fit of temper," the young woman said.

When he heard that his wife would never be able
to scold him again, Rip felt better.
Now an old woman came up to him out of the crowd
and took him by the hand.
"Yes, I know you. You really are Rip van Winkle.
Welcome back, neighbour.
Where have you been for these last twenty years?"

R
IP TOLD THE CROWD HIS EXTRAORDINARY STORY,
about the strange old men playing ninepins,
about the barrel of wine,
and how it had seemed to him that he had spent
no more than one night in the mountains.
Then the oldest man in the village nodded his head
"I have heard stories like this before.
My old grandfather told me that
every twenty years our ancestor, Hendrick Hudson,
comes back to these mountains to look after his people.
My own father once saw him,
and heard the thunder of the ninepin balls."

AFTER THIS, RIP VAN WINKLE LIVED IN HIS DAUGHTER'S HOUSE, and played with her children.
And today, when thunder rolls round the Catskill mountains, people look up from their work and nod to each other and say, "They're playing ninepins up there again."